Catching a
STORYFISH

Catching a
STORYFISH

JANICE N. HARRINGTON

WORDƒONG

AN IMPRINT OF HIGHLIGHTS

Honesdale, Pennsylvania

This is a work of fiction. Names, characters, places, and incidents are products
of the author's imagination or are used fictitiously. Any resemblance to actual
events, locales, or persons, living or dead, is entirely coincidental.

WordSong
An Imprint of Highlights
815 Church Street
Honesdale, Pennsylvania 18431
wordsongpoetry.com
Printed in the United States of America

ISBN: 978-1-62979-429-7 (hardcover)
ISBN: 978-1-62979-743-4 (e-book)
Library of Congress Control Number: 2016936167

First edition
10 9 8 7 6 5 4 3 2 1

Design by Barbara Grzeslo
Production by Sue Cole
The text is set in Garamond 3.
The titles are set in Buckley.

For Grandpa Elmer and Alyssa,
and for our poet, Katharen

CONTENTS

9

PROLOGUE

THE STORYFISH

Grandpa says
it's the storyfish
that fills me
with stories to tell,

a storyfish
all rainbow-colored
and quick, quick,
a storyfish that's guppy-small
and sometimes as big as a whale.

It leaps and plunges
and dives down deep,
and swims inside my dreams.

I have a storyfish
inside me, a fish
made of words.
It nibbles, nibbles
when I'm daydreaming.

But if I'm quiet, if I listen hard,
I'll hear the storyfish,
and it will tell me
the best story ever.

Listen, and you'll hear it too.

Chapter 1

THE
BIG
MISTAKE

KEET-KEET PARAKEET

"You'd talk the whiskers off a catfish,"
Grandpa says, "and the shine
off a new penny."

"Grab the glue, grab the tape,"
Daddy says. "Keet, if you keep talking,
I'll need to stick on an extra pair of ears."

They're right. I like to talk.
I like to spin stories,
this-is-what-I-did stories,
this-is-what-I-saw stories,
stories to make my brother giggle-bouncy
and wiggly as a worm,
stories to make Daddy lean in
and hold me octopus-tight,
stories to make Mama's eyes
shine birthday-candle bright.

My teacher used to say,
"Katharen, that's a good story.
But why don't we give someone else a turn?"
I think she meant I'd said enough.

My grandma used to say,
"Only thing wrong with a duck is its bill."
I think she meant I go *quack-quack-quack*.

But Mama says, "Keet,
you're a born storyteller.
You're my little parakeet.
You always have something to say."

That's why my friends call me
"Keet-Keet Parakeet,
that story-talking, story-making girl."

WHAT I TRIED TO SAY

At least—
I used to be.

I talk, talk, talked,

but this time no one listened.
This time, it didn't matter

what I had to say.

Mama and Daddy moved us away.
Even though I talked,

even though I squawked
and told them that I had to stay.

THE NEW HOUSE

When we moved in,
Daddy said
the small red-brick house
with the long gray driveway,
the peely-paint fence,
and the rickety picnic table
was our new home.

When we moved in,
the neighbors stopped to stare.
A girl watched from the alley.
Then she sat on the curb
and scribble-scribbled in a notebook.
(What was she doing?)

When we moved in,
my daddy said, "Keet-Keet,
what do you think?"

I frowned.
I think we made a big mistake.

WHAT ALLEGRA SAW

A new family.
A girl.
A boy.
But
I didn't see
any pets.

I saw
one bicycle,
one tricycle,
three beds,
a long sofa,
a desk,
shelves,
an old clock,
a dining room table,
and four fat chairs.

I saw
boxes—
bulging boxes,
boxes tall and boxes short,
boxes labeled,
tied with string,
boxes filled
with a thousand things.

I saw
the new girl look
at me,
but she didn't smile.
She didn't wave.
She didn't come over.

Maybe   she's shy.

Maybe   she's stuck-up?

Maybe   she's m-e-a-n?

DO WE HAVE TO?

Do we have to stay?
Mama turns sad eyes to me.
Can't we just go back?

Do we have to stay?
Daddy sighs and rubs his head.
Can't we just go back?

Do we have to stay?
Do we *really* have to stay?
What if I go back?

GO PLAY

"Stay out of the way, Keet,"
Mama says.

"Go play with Noah in the backyard,"
Daddy says.

"Where are we going, Keet-y?"

"Come on, Nose," I say.

"Are you going to play with me?"
Nose asks. "Can we play ball?"

"Come on, Nose."
Nosy Nose, Nosy Noah,
full-of-questions, full-of-why,
full-of-when, my nosy-posy
little brother.
"Hurry up, Nose."

Nose skips toward the back fence,
bouncing his ball.

He watches the neighbor girl
turn cartwheels on the grassy hem.
She stops. She looks at us.

"You want to play ball?" Nose says.

The neighbor girl says nothing.
She throws her hands to the ground,
pushes her legs over her head,
and wheels away.

"Keet-y, why won't she play with us?"

I think about CarlAlishaMichaelDante
LilyKeishaGordonEvieMadisonEmma
CharletteTaylor and all my friends.
I think about hunting for muscadines.
I think about fish fries and laughter.
I think about playing checkers with my uncle
    and winning sometimes.
I think about the tear in my teacher's eye
when she said, "Good-bye, Katharen, good-bye."

Why did we move here?
Why? Why? Why?

WHY?

Better job,
better pay,
better school,
away, away.

For Grandpa's sake. He's all alone.
For all the reasons parents drone,
for all the reasons parents say,
for bigger dreams, for better dreams,
we moved away.

A BOX BIG ENOUGH

Please, give me a box
to pack my cousins in,
a box to hold the wide front porch
        where I liked to sit and swing,
a box for the fishpond and another for the fish,
a box for my old room
        and my old floor that c-r-e-a-k-e-d,
a box for the egg-gold evenings
when all my friends played tag.
        And we ran, ran, ran, pinwheeling
brown legs, swinging
brown arms, laughing and calling,
running this way and that, trying not to be,
        not to be, not to be—it!
We played long enough for the stars to join in,
        for the moon to shine as bright as the eyes
of my cousin Carl who almost, almost, almost
tagged me—but I escaped!

Give me a box,
a cardboard box, a wide box, a deep box
for the long, low screech of the swing on the porch,
for Mama and Daddy softly talking,
with Noah on Mama's lap
and me in the middle.

Give me a box,
a big box,
the right box, a heart box,
to carry everything I love
and all my friends
from far, far away.

SETTLING IN #1

"I know it's hard to move away, Keet,"
Daddy says. "I miss our home
and our friends too."

"You do, Daddy?"

He doesn't answer. Instead he lifts
his shovel and drives it into the hard
ground again, digging, digging, digging.

"Does his talking with his eyes," Mama always says.
"Why take a thousand words, when one look will do?"

The shovel *chuh-chuh-chuhh*s.
Heaves of dirt fall
in clumps atop the grass.

"I promised your mama a garden
and an apple tree," Daddy says.

Daddy wants me to help.
I put on Mama's garden gloves and my purple floppy hat.
Nose comes too. Nosy nuisance.

In a corner of the yard, Daddy digs
the hole, deep and wide.
It smells earthy and wormy.
It smells rotty and sweet.
He fills the hole with manure
and mulch to help the tree grow.

"Smells bad," Nose says.
The corners of Daddy's eyes crinkle,
and he nods at Nose.

Daddy lets us pull the burlap wrapping
from the apple tree. Then he
gently loosens the curling roots.

"See the roots, Noah?" Daddy says. "Tree
has to have roots, if it's going to grow."

Noah stoops down and looks.
The roots look twiggy and tangled,
crooked-fingered and stringy.

"Rooooots," Nose chants.
"Root, root, root."

"Strong roots, strong tree," Daddy says.
"The tree has to get settled in,
and these roots will help it grow."
Daddy watches me then.
His eyes seem like two earthy holes,
where you could plant something
to root and grow strong.

Do I have roots?
Maybe Mama, Daddy, and Nose are my roots.
Maybe I'm a root too. Maybe.

"Strong roots, strong tree," I say.

Daddy's eyes hold me for a while.
He nods, but he doesn't say anything.
He asks me to hold the tree in place
while he covers the roots with dirt.
Roots in a new place, settling in.

ONE THING ONLY

Mama says,
"Look on the bright side."

There isn't any.

Mama says,
"Count your blessings."

Zero.

Mama says,
"Every rain cloud has a silver lining."

Where? Show me one.

Mama says,
"Keet, you will find something good here,
if you look hard enough."

I try, try, try,
but I can see only one good thing: Grandpa!

EVERY FRIDAY, I CALL GRANDPA

Keet: Grandpa, what are you doing?

Grandpa: Doing? I'm talking to you.

Keet: Grandpa, you want to go fishing?

Grandpa: *Wishing?* Well, I wish I could take a good nap.

Keet: No, Grandpa, not wishing—*fishing.*
            Do you want to go fishing?

Grandpa: Hissing? No, I don't hear anything hissing.

Keet: No, Grandpa. Fishing! Do you want to go *fishing?*

Grandpa: Is this my Fish Bait talking or some ol' snake?

Keet: Grandpa, you're just being silly. I want to go fishing.

Grandpa: You wanna go fishing?

Keet: Yes, Grandpa.

Grandpa: Well, isn't that something.
            I was just thinking about doing a little fishing.
            Would you like to go?

Keet: Yes, Grandpa.

YOU'RE A WIGGLE WORM

"Can I go, Keet-y?"

"No. Just me and Grandpa."

"Why can't I go?" Nose says.

"You're too small," I say.
"A catfish might eat you."

"Can't I go to Grandpa's house?"

"No, not this time."

"Why can't I go?"

"You wiggle too much.
Grandpa might think you're a worm.
He'll put you in his tackle box
and use you for bait,
and then a catfish will eat you for sure."

"I don't want a catfish to eat me.
Keet-y, tell Grandpa I'm not a worm."

"Grandpa can't help it.
He likes catfish.
And you'd make a good worm.
A really, really big catfish
will eat all your toes,
and tickle you
with its catfish whiskers, like this."

"No! Keet-y, noooooo!
I'm not a worm!"

"Yes," I say. And I chase him
all over the house.

"Catfish tickles!
Catfish tickles!
Wiggly Nose
gets catfish tickles!"

GRAB THE TACKLE BOX!

Now that we moved
I go fishing with Grandpa
not just on summer visits,
not just on his trips back home,
but every Saturday.
"We'll go rain or shine
or sweet potato," Grandpa says.
He picks me up in his truck, Big Blue,
and we ride bumping up and down the road
looking for the best fishing holes.

I'm Grandpa's fishing buddy.
He calls me "Fish Bait." But
when I talk too much and
scare the fish, he calls me
"some 70 pounds of trouble."

On Fishing Days, we grab
        Grandpa's tackle box.
        It has fishing line, sinkers, bobbins, pliers, and bait.
We grab   our fishing hats and mud boots.
We grab   fishing poles, buckets, lunch sacks,
        peanutbutterdillpickle sandwiches,
        and mud juice (that's what we call chocolate milk),
        and lots and lots and lots of marshmallows.

Sometimes, Grandpa builds a fire.
We melt marshmallows and eat them

ooey-gooey on the end of a stick.
Sometimes, we nibble them—fat, soft,
and sugar-dusty—from the tip of a straw.
I call them marshmallow mops.
Grandpa says, "*Mm-mm-mm*,
my belly had one empty spot left
but I think that put a plug in it."

JUST THE RIGHT SPOT

We stomp through fields and weeds.
We swing our buckets back and forth.
We step-step-high and step-step-low
while Grandpa looks for a good spot to fish.
"Catfish like places to hide," Grandpa says.
"They like still and slow and muddy."

Grandpa knows my tongue
is wiggly as a wiggle worm
and quick as a mosquito,
so wherever we look, he says, "*Shhhhhh.
Shhhhh*. The fish will hear you."

"Really, Grandpa?"

"Yes," he whispers.
"They'll hear your heart beating through the fishing line,
hear your heels hard-thumping on the bank,
hear your bottom bouncing and wriggling all around.

"*Shhhhhh*, Fish Bait,
            shhhhhh."

FISH BAIT

Grandpa baits his fishing hook,
and then he tries to bait mine.

He plucks a worm out of a coffee tin.

    "No, Grandpa, too tickly."

He pushes a dough ball
from a plastic sack.

    "No, Grandpa, too stinky."

He pulls a froggy-kind-of-thingy
from his tackle box.

    "No, Grandpa, too rubbery-slippery."

"Well, Fish Bait,
how do you plan to catch a fish?"

I rub my nose and think a bit.
Then I look in my lunch sack.

"Marshmallow, Grandpa!
I'll bait my hook with a marshmallow."

F
I
S
H
I
N
G

L
I
N
E

K
N
O
T

H
O
O
K

Marshmallowmarshmellow
mellowmarshmellowmarsh
marshlowmarshmellmarshy
marshsweetsmellowsweets
mooooshysmoooshymarshy
mellowmallowmarshmellow

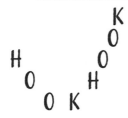

FISHING LESSON #1

"You need to think like a fish," Grandpa says,
"if you're going to hook a fish.

"And the only way to think like a catfish
is to listen. Catfish are great listeners."

"Catfish don't have ears, Grandpa."

"Yes, they do, Fish Bait.
Yes, they do.

"Sound slips through their bodies
like water and tickles their bladder,
and tickles their bones,
and tickles their inside ears," Grandpa says.

"If those catfish hear a wiggly-giggly girl,
a wiggly-giggly, can't-sit-still,
word-buzzy girl, they'll hide
double-quick and sink down in the mud.

"To catch a fish," Grandpa says,
"you've got to sit quiet and hold still.
You've got to listen, really listen
with your inside ears."

"Inside ears, Grandpa?"

"That's right, Fish Bait. Deep inside
where no one else can see 'em."

"Is that true, Grandpa?"
But all he says is,

"Shhhhhhhhhhhhhh."

FISHING LESSON #2

Shhhhhhh. The leaves rub,
the leaves rustle.

Grandpa's breath
scrapes in and out.

Water slicks and licks the bank.

Frogs drum *ah-RUM-ah-RUM*,
dragonflies *zummmm*,
mosquitoes *zeeee*,
blue-bottomed flies go *zzu*,
and *zzu*, and *zzzzzu*.

Splish!
          Plop!

Splash!

I'm a catfish girl floating above deep, cool mud,
catfish quiet, catfish still.
I'm a catfish listening with my whole body.

BEDTIME STORIES

"Listen," Nose says.
"Listen, Keet-y, listen to me tell it:
Oogle-oogle-oogle go away!"

Nose screws his face tight.
He looks monster-mean.
He shows his claws.

He says, "I'm going to chomp
and chomp and chew you up!
Tell me the story, Keet-y."

"Not now, Nose."

"Pleeeeease!" Nose says.

"If I tell you, will you go to bed?"

"Yes," Nose says.

"Promise?"

"Yes," Nose says.
"Tell me the story,
and make me chocolate milk,
and read to me, and then
tell me another story,
and then I'll go to sleep."

Little brothers make a lot of trouble.

KEET'S STORY FOR NOAH

Once upon a time, there was a little boy
who really, really liked chocolate milk.

One night, he went into the kitchen
to get chocolate milk in his favorite cup
covered with great big blue dinosaurs.

He had just poured a super-gigantic cup
of chocolate milk
when he heard something right behind him.

            "The Oogle Monster!" Nose says.

"Yes," I say, "the Oogle Monster."

And the Oogle Monster
said in his oogle-oogle voice:

"I'm going to chomp and stomp
and chew you up!"

            "Chew you up," Nose says. "Chew you up!"

The little boy did not want to be eaten.
He wanted to drink his chocolate milk
in his super-gigantic cup with blue dinosaurs.

So he said in a loud voice,
"Oogle-oogle-oogle, go away!"

The Oogle Monster
had never heard such a loud voice.
It made him tremble.
It made him shake.
He covered his ears—
and then he stuck his head through the kitchen floor.

The little boy started to tiptoe,
tiptoe, tiptoe back toward his bed.

But once more he heard something
right behind him.

It was the Oogle Monster,
and the Oogle Monster
said, "I'm going to chomp and stomp
and chew you up!"

The little boy didn't want to be eaten.
He wanted to drink his chocolate milk.
So he said in a soft, soft voice,
"Oogle-oogle-oogle, *go away!"*

The Oogle Monster
had never heard such a soft, sweet voice.
It made him yawn.
It made him fall fast asleep
right on top of the kitchen floor.

"And he snored really loud," Nose says.

"Yes, he did."

"And the little boy's mother came,"
Nose says.

"Yes, she did."

The mother said, "Oogle-oogle-oogle, go away!"
And she swept the Oogle Monster up,
and washed him down the sink.

Nose laughs and laughs.
"She washed the monster down the sink!"
he says.

I pour icy-cold chocolate milk
into his big blue dinosaur cup.

And Nose drinks it up, up, up—
and burps!

FISHING LESSON #3

In bed at night, I listen.
I pretend
I'm a night catfish.

I pretend
the stars are catfish looking down
and listening.

I hear my baby brother
singing *Oogle-oogle.*

I hear Mama and Daddy
talking low.

I hear the moths flutter-beat
against the window.

I hear the door of my room quietly open
and feel Mama's breath against my cheek
and Daddy tuck-tucking my blanket.

"Sweet dreams," Mama says.
"Night-night, Keet," Daddy says.

I try to listen with my inside ear,
and I hear the worry in Mama's voice.
She wants me to be happy here.

I listen with my inside ear,
and I hear long roads in Daddy's voice.
He's working hard for us. He's working hard for me.

Their voices swim inside of me
like silvery fish, until I fall asleep.

NEW SCHOOL

Down in my stomach
I feel grasshoppers, tadpoles,
and the silvery minnows that dart
and swim beside the bank.

Down in my stomach
I feel wiggly worms and eels.
Monday, I'm going to a new school.
Mama says it's a small school, a good school.
But I'll be the new kid.

Down in my stomach
I feel bubbling and sinking.
In a few days, I'll learn new names
and new faces, go to new classes
with new teachers, new
rooms, and new desks.
And I'll be the new kid.

Down in my stomach
I feel a question
like a pointy fishhook:
What if I don't like it?

Chapter 2

FIRST WEEK: WHY DO YOU TALK THAT WAY?

BELLS

Feet pounding,
laughter rising,
words flying,
kids flocking.

Bells.

Pencils dropping,
buses stopping,
moms pecking kiss, kiss,
dads squeezing hug, hug,
big kids,
little kids.

Bells.

Principal pacing
back
and forth,
teachers talking,
fast walking,
doors opening,
doors closing.

Bells.

Desks screeching,
chairs scraping,
PA squawking,
janitor mopping.

Bells.

Kids in lines,
kids in bunches,
quiet kids, loud kids,
kids chasing,
kids running,
kids yelling,

Bells.

WHAT ALLEGRA THOUGHT

Nobody's quiet. Everyone's talking,
everyone except
                    the New Girl.
The kids look at her
the way they looked at me
when I was new.

I wonder what she's like.
I wonder what she likes to do.

I draw her five pigtails.
I draw her socks—blue with pink hearts.
I draw her great big eyes,
New-Kid Eyes that look at everything
and seem s-c-a-r-e-d.

FISHHOOK EYES

Their eyes look like pencil points.
Their eyes go scribble, scribble
and poke, poke.
Their eyes are fishhooks.

"Class, this is Katharen Walker.
Katharen, can you tell us
where you went to school before?"

"Vernon Elementary School," I say.

A boy in the front row laughs.
A girl says, "You sound funny."

"And where is that, Katharen?"

I didn't know
that words could have hard edges.
I didn't know that words
could get stuck in your throat.

"In . . . Alabamer," I say.
But I don't say it very loud,
and the teacher asks me to repeat it.

"Alabamer."

"Alabama? Very good. Welcome
to your new school, Katharen.
I have friends from the South,
and I'll look forward to learning
more about you."

"Yes, Ma'am," I whisper,
but already I can tell that I made
another mistake.
Nobody says that here.

I feel their eyes again.
Their eyes are sharp teeth
that want to gnaw
and nibble me away.

MONDAY:
READING AND WRITING CENTERS

I like to roll words in my mouth, like pebbles.
I like to read my books aloud.
I like the way stories unwind like Grandpa's fishing line.
I like the way a good story puts pictures in my head
and little minnow-thoughts that dart and swim and wiggle.
I like to pretend I'm the hero with a magic sword,
or a Snow Queen, or a traveler from a faraway star.
I act out every part and every part is me.
My old teacher said, "Katharen, you were made for the stage."
My new teacher says, "Katharen, why don't you try again on the
  next page?"

YELLA? YELLOW?

"That's not right.
That's not how you say it,"
John Royale says.

"She said *yella*, Ms. Harner.
Tell her
that's not the way you say *yellow*."

"John," Ms. Harner says,
"why don't you read the next paragraph?
Thank you, Katharen, you read well."

But the other kids giggle.
They giggle when I say *yella*.
They giggle when I talk.

"Katharen Walker,
you're a funny talker," they say.
"Why do you talk that way?"

RECESS

Girls on the monkey bars,
girls in circles,
girls in knots,

girls jump-jumping
under the basketball hoop,
girls that miss and skip and bounce and—oops!

Girls blowing bubblegum,
girls braiding hair,
girls chanting, "Dare! Dare!
Double-dare!"

Girl talk, girl telling,
girls whispering girl secrets.
Girl strut and girl sass—

      but

—I'm by myself,
a fish flopping on a sandbar,
my thoughts turning in a circle,
my tongue tied in a knot.

STINGS

Chloe whispers, "This isn't the South."
Then she calls me 'Bama Mouth.

In math, no one wants to be my study buddy,
and Keith won't share the book with me.

John Royale giggles. "Glad I'm not like you,
or I'd have that funny accent too."

I pretend to erase their words away.
I pretend I can't hear the things they say.

But sometimes, the mean is a bumblebee.
It buzzes and stings inside of me.

NOT YET

That clock is a snail.
Snail, I want to go home now.
Move fast, Snail. Move fast!

SCHOOL'S OUT!

I put my books away
I put my homework away.
I put my backpack on my back.
I put my hat on my head.

But where should I put

   'Bama Mouth!
   Katharen's got a 'Bama mouth!

Where should I put

   kids staring at me,
   kids laughing at me,
   kids saying, "You talk funny."

Where should I put

   the madsadbad
   of being new?

When you're not like them,
and they're not like you.

Inside, question marks snag
and pull like fishhooks.
Why can't they like me?
Why don't they?
Why won't they?

I WONDER HOW SHE KNOWS?

Door—SLAMMED!
Books dropped,
shoes kicked, one by one,
homework flung.

Stomp! Stomp!
Doorknob—yank.
SLAM!

Bed crash,
pillow smash,
crab-crawling beneath the sheet,
body squeezed into a knot.

Quiet knock,
door squeak,
soft steps,
bed creak,
fingers circling circles on my back,
covers slipped below my head,

a warm face
against my cheek.
Mama's voice:
"First days are hard, Keet.
Do you want to tell me about it?"

NOTHING TO SAY

I used to be Keet-Keet Parakeet.
I used to talk to anyone.
I used to talk anywhere.

But now at school,
words are peanut-butter sticky
and tight as lids on pickle jars.

I used to talk
from morning till night.

But now at school,
words are pretzel-crooked.
They never come out right.

I used to be Keet-Keet Parakeet.
I used to be.
I used to be.

KIDS SAY

"Grandpa, the kids say I talk funny.
They laugh at my words.
They're mean, Grandpa. And I don't like,
I don't like, I don't like school at all.

"Can't let the mosquitoes bother you, Fish Bait,
not if you want to catch a fish."

"Grandpa, stop talking about fishing.
I'm talking about school."

"Well, fish swim in schools. Don't they?"

GRANDPA FRIDAYS

"Grandpa, there's a girl in my class,
and she doesn't make fun of me
like the other kids, but she
keeps staring at me and she won't talk."

"Let the fish come to you," Grandpa says.
"Some fish just like to take their time, Fish Bait."

"Grandpa, she's not a fish."

"Notafish?
What kind of fish is that?
Heard of a catfish, a sunfish, a dogfish.
Can't say I've heard of a notafish."

"Grandpa!"

WHAT DO YOU SAY, GRANDPA?

Keet: Let's go fishing, Grandpa.

Grandpa: With who?

Keet: With me.

Grandpa: With you? Where are you going?

Keet: I'm going fishing.

Grandpa: You are? Well, why don't you take me with you?

Keet: Grandpa, why are you sooooooo silly?

WE'RE GOING AFTER OL' MUDDY JOE

"Ol' Muddy Joe is a catfish.
He's older than mud.
He's got whiskers as long
as the Mississippi," Grandpa says.

"Really, Grandpa, really?"

Grandpa says, "Ol' Muddy Joe
is quick and strong as flood water.
He's the smartest catfish ever.
He teaches all the other fish in his catfish school
to break fishing line, spit out hooks,
and drive fishermen crazy. Ol' Muddy Joe
is wily and tricky and sneaky too."

"Really, Grandpa, really?"

"Ol' Muddy Joe lies on the river bottom
in his electric catfish suit.
He can taste the water, taste the land.
Taste how humans have changed the taste of things.
He's listening to me talking right now,
and he's laughing his old catfish laugh."

"Really, Grandpa, really?"

"Well, maybe not a laugh.
But he sure is smiling: all catfish smile.
One of these days, I'm going to catch him
and pat him on his big yellow belly."

"Really, Grandpa, really?"

"Gonna try. He's fooled me a time or two.
Raced ahead and snagged my line.
He's slipped off my hook and put a minnow on instead.
But we've got an understanding, that old fish and me.
Been talking to one another a real long time.
That fish can tell you all kinds of stories."

"Really, Grandpa, really?"

MUDDY JOE

We bait our hooks and sit quiet
beside the slow muddy water.
Grandpa lifts his line and flicks it out.
The pole's red bobbin floats
like a bright berry, and the line hangs
like a spider's web, like ice-colored string.

We wait and wait,
until waiting feels like
mosquito humming, like
thick gooey mud, like
slow-moving water. I wait
and Grandpa waits.

Sunfish, bluegill, bass, and perch,
but no catfish and no Ol' Muddy Joe.

"Looks like Ol' Muddy's not coming, Grandpa."
Grandpa lifts his cap and rubs his head.
"No, Ol' Muddy's not in a talking mood, I guess.
But we're not giving up, Fish Bait.
We're not giving in, are we?"

"No, Grandpa.
We're not giving up."

CAN WE CATCH HIM?

Grandpa baits his hook and throws it out.
We wait so long that I fall asleep on Grandpa's shoulder.
Grandpa gives me a nudge. He points.

Bob
          bob
                    bob.

The bobbin dips down and up, down and up.
"*Shhhh*," Grandpa whispers.
I hold my breath.

Grandpa yanks on the fishing pole.
The tip of the pole curls downward.
The fishing line reeeeeeeeels out.
A huge catfish beats and thrashes
against the water.

"Is it Ol' Muddy Joe? Is it Ol' Muddy?"

"Sure is, Fish Bait. It sure is!"

"Pull, Grandpa, pull!"
I grab Grandpa's waist and try to help him pull.
Grandpa leans back and the fish rises
from the muddy deep, up, up, up,
and rolls, and splashes back again.

"Come on, you ol' rascal," Grandpa shouts.
"Come on, Muddy Joe," I shout.
ZZZZZZZ the line reels out, out, out—

and then: *Snap!*

                                  Splash!

        Plonk!

                                              Gone!

JUST US

No worries.
No itchy, buzzy
school troubles.

Why can't we
always be this way?

NOSE TROUBLE

"Go away, Nose."
"No."

"Nose, go away," I say.
"No."

"Nose, leave me alone!"
"No."

"Stop acting silly, Nose."

"Silly, silly," Nose says.

"And get out of my room," I say.

"Read to me, Keet-y."

"Nose, go away."

Nose scurries away and then comes back
with his stuffed chicken and his favorite book,
Where the Wild Things Are.

"No, Nose."

"Yes!"

"No, Nose."

"Yes!"

Nose wrinkles up his nose.
He sniffles,
he snuffles,
and then he starts to whimper.
He throws himself
on the carpet to cry.

"Keet, what's wrong with Noah?"
Mama calls.

"Nothing, he just wants a book."

"Can you read him one, Keet?
I'm trying to get the laundry done."

Nose looks at me.
He smiles and holds up his book.

"Keet?" Mama calls again.

I look at Nose.
"You're nothing but trouble," I say.

Nose smiles.
"I'm a wild thing," he says. *"Grrrrrrr."*

THINGS TO DO WITH A BABY BROTHER

1. Eat him for supper on buttered toast.
2. Ship him to Siberia, parcel post.
3. Sell him at a lemonade stand.
4. Leave him for the garbage man.
5. Wrap him in newspaper and seal him with tape.
6. Put him in the zoo with a big hairy ape.
7. Roll him up like a jelly roll.
8. Hide him away in a deep deep hole.
9. Go fishing for tuna and use him for bait,
10. or mix him in the batter for his birthday cake.

THE YELLOW KITE

The park buzzes
with mamas and daddies,
with brothers and sisters,
with babies,
with picnics,
with dog walkers,
with long-legged bicyclists
and huff-puffy joggers.

The park shines
with kite flyers
and all kinds of kites:

box-shaped,
        diamond-shaped,
                caterpillar-shaped,
kites shaped
        like dragonflies,
                and kites with long,
                        snaky tails.

Nose and I have a kite too.
I made it from yellow paper,
and tape, and drinking straws.
I made it in school.
It has a long, long string
wrapped around a popsicle stick.

It's not a big kite.
It's not a fancy kite.
It's not a store-bought kite.
It isn't shaped like a dragon, or a fish, or a butterfly.

Nose looks at our little kite.
He looks at the fancy kites.
He looks at the wide, high sky.

"Will it fly?"
"Yes," I say. "I made a good kite."

I hold the kite above my head.
I run, run, run. The kite jumps. It spins.
It spins around, around, and then it
                    drops.

Our kite looks like melted butter in the grass.
Maybe it wasn't a good kite.
Maybe it can't fly.

"Try again," Nose says.

We climb to the top of the hill and wait.
We watch the other kites.

Then I feel the air stroke my cheek.
I feel the wind tug my braids.
I hold the kite high above my head.
I run and toss the kite even higher.

"Run!" Nose shouts. "Run fast!"

I run fast, fast, fast until I feel the wind
snatch the kite and steal it away.
The wind plays tug-of-war with me.
The wind rolls my kite across the sky
like a yellow crayon.

"It's flying! It's flying!
Let me hold it! Let me hold it!"

I hold the string for a long while
because I am the big sister,
and it's my kite.

Then I give it to Nose.
I let him run with it.
I let him circle it around and around.

Our kite flies as high
as the fancy kites (almost),
as high as the big kites (almost).

Our kite flies and plays with us
until the wind softens,
and sighs,
and whispers away.

Then our kite falls
like a flashing comet,
like a splash of lemonade.

The yellow paper rips.
The kite won't fly anymore.

"It was a good kite," Nose says.
"Make another one."

TOGETHER

"Can you take another one
for supper?" Grandpa asks.

"Only if it's you," Mama says.

"We're eating elephant spaghetti," Nose says.
"We're eating snail rumps," I say.
"Is that all?" Grandpa says.
"Snail rumps are pretty small."

"Noooo, Grandpa," I say.
"We're also having—
monkey toes and pigweed,
cowboy boots boiled in butter,
elbow pudding, goose teeth,
fishhead scramble, worm meat,
bedbug biscuits, frog-juice jelly,
and Mama's baking all of us in a pie."

"Sounds good," Grandpa says, "and it smells
so sweet your mama must have stuck
her toe in it. If you bring me a big bowlful
of that fishhead scramble, Noah, I'll stay
for breakfast in the morning."

"We don't have any fishheads!" Nose giggles.

"Well, some of that pie then, with all of us in it.
I'm sure that will be just as good."

And it was good,
Mama, Daddy, Grandpa, Nose, and Me,
a family pie, an all-of-us-together pie.

THE BEDTIME BELL

"Another one! Another one!"
Nose shouts.

Grandpa gives Nose
another piggyback ride
and carries him down
the hall to Nose's room.
Grandpa swoops Nose up
and flops him dowwwn into bed.

"Good night, sleep tight.
Don't let those fishes bite,"
Grandpa says, wiggling
Nose's pudgy fat toe.

"Ready, Fish Bait?"

"Ready, Grandpa."

Grandpa and I march to my room.
When he hugs me, I feel
his rough whiskers. I smell
the coffee on his breath.
He cups my head in his hands.
My grandpa's hands are soft,
but he has a scar where a fishhook
caught him once.

His eyes are like muddy water.

"Good night, sleep tight.
Don't let those fishes bite,"
Grandpa says, wobbling my nose.

"Grand-ba! Let go by doze!"

He laughs and kisses me, again.
Grandpa's laugh is like a bell.
I hear it ringing in my sleep.

Chapter 3

SECOND WEEK: NEW-GIRL BLUES

NEW-GIRL BLUES

I got the New-Girl blues.
I got those back-to-school and don't-want-to,
do-I-have-to-Mama? do-I-have-to? blues.

Blues in my thinking, blues
in my walk. Blue and lonely lonely
because of my New-Girl talk.

I got the New-Girl,
don't-want-to-go,
don't-make-me-go blues.

SPELLING ON M-O-N-D-A-Y

In spelling, we line up to play baseball.
The teacher divides us into four teams
and pairs one team against another.
Each pair of teams takes a turn
while the teacher pitches words.

My team doesn't do so well.

Chloe smirks when I spell p-e-n-c-i-l.
"I'm surprised you can spell it," she whispers.
"You don't even know how to say it.
It's *pencil*, 'Bama Mouth, not *pancil*."
I ignore her, but I strike out anyway,
when I can't spell w-e-i-r-d.
John Royale sticks his tongue out at me.
Allegra rolls her eyes at him.

Then only two teams are left.

John Royale's team is good.
But they strike out until he
is the only one left.

Then John Royale stumbles on astronauts.
He says, "a-s-t-r-o-n-o-t-s."

Next Allegra's team is up.
"A-s-t-r-o-n-a-u-t-s," Allegra says,
and she moves to first base.

The teacher keeps pitching words.
John Royale's team is ahead on points.
Allegra's team needs two more runs.

But two of her teammates strike out.
Only four kids are left.

After Sonya spells *p-r-a-i-r-i-e*,
and Hudson spells *I-l-l-i-n-o-i-s*,
and Mark spells *n-e-i-g-h-b-o-r-h-o-o-d*,
the score is tied!
The bases are loaded.
Allegra's team whoops and cheers.
John Royale groans.

"Batter up!" Ms. Harner says.
It's Allegra's turn again.
She looks unstoppable.
She looks like she can't possibly lose.

Sonya and Gabby say
"Come on, Allegra!"

John Royale's team leans in close.
John Royale whispers *miss, miss, miss*.
His team puts on You'll-Never-Beat-Us faces.

Ms. Harner runs her finger down the page.
She picks a word, a hard word,
a word that no one wants to spell.

"*Entwined*," Ms. Harner says.
"I entwined two pieces of string to make a rope."

"Entwined? Entwined?" we all think.

"Entwined," Allegra says.

E   Are you sure it's not I?

N   Yes, definitely N.

T   No, another N.

W   W, there's a W?

I   Okay, I.

N   Now another N.

E   Nooooo, N another N!

D   Well, that's right anyway.

"We win! We win!" John Royale shouts,
and his team begins to cheer.

Allegra's team crosses their fingers
and squinches their faces tight.
But how can her spelling possibly be right?
Everyone stares at Ms. Harner.

Ms. Harner closes the book with a clap.
"Correct!" she says.

Allegra gives us a thumbs-up,
but she doesn't smile.

ALLEGRA CAN SPELL ANYTHING

Baloney, balloon, or boogaloo,
Concert,
Dictionary,
Eclipse, éclair, electricity,
Finicky, filigree, frail,
Give her the
Hardest, most
Irregular, most brain-
Jamming, old-fashioned,
Kid-stumping,
Longer-than-a-yardstick,
Multi-million-syllables, or trillion-billion-vowel word—

and it won't matter.

Nothing's too hard,
Or odd or off-base, too
Peculiar,
Quirky, quizzical, or
Rare.
She can spell the
Toughest, the terrifying, the totally
Unusual, the wackiest, and
Very most vexing and
Weirdest of words, like xaphoon,
Xerox, or xerography, and she always gets them right.

Yikes! She even takes our challenge and spells

Hippopotomonstrosesquipedalian.

"Zowie! What a zinger!" she says,
zipping her lips with a zesty zip
to show that she is done.

WEIRD

When we're done with baseball,
I tell Allegra that she's a good speller.
"*Entwined* was really hard," I say.

"W-E-I-R-D," she says.

I think she means that's how you spell it.
I don't *think* she means me.
But she doesn't smile, so it's hard to tell.

ALLEGRA WONDERS

Why is she smiling?
Does she want to be my friend?
Should I talk to her?

KEET WONDERS

Why doesn't she smile?
Does she want to be my friend?
Should I talk to her?

MATH CLASS

Long Divi4sion, arith88metic,
subtracti2on, and multip9lication:

numbers tumble
and spin in my head.

I have numbers blizzarding
in my 5brain, and numbers
storming behind my eyes4.

I try to do what the teacher
says, but the numbers won't
hold sti567ll. They get all mixed
up with everything and spill out
everywhere. I have numbers
tangled in my braid9s, numbers
caught between my t2eeth,
4, 5, 6, and 7 stuck to my tongue,
and 177 tickling my nose.

Now the number blizzard
is a thunder2storm. I've got a number
tornado turning, tur3ning, tur3ning
in my brain, a number earthquake
breaking up my thoug7hts.

Letters and numbers
are tum7bling and churn44ing,
swirling and swimm99ing.

I can't sort the numbers out
or tell the words a3part.

I want to shout *STOP!*
Stop spinning. Be still!

But only 0 comes out.

CAFETERIA

Cheesy pizza smell.
Grab the trays and lunch boxes.
We can't wait to eat.

In the school cafeteria, I get my tray, and Ms. Scott reminds us to sit with our class, but when I get near the table no one moves over. The girls all sit with girls. The boys all sit with boys. Everyone stares at me. John Royale makes a face. I don't know where to sit. Allegra sits next to Sonya and Gabby. I see them talking, but Allegra scooches over so that I can sit beside her, and I do. I see her looking at my cookie. It is a good cookie. It is a super-extra tummy-yummy gooey-with-chocolate cookie. I want it, but I am being nice since she was nice to me. So I put the cookie on her tray. Allegra takes it and mumbles "anks." I smile at her again to show her I am being nice. But she doesn't smile back. She eats my whole cookie, and doesn't give me any of it.

WEDNESDAY:
LIBRARY

Today, the class gets to spend
a whole *hour* in the library.
We can read whatever we want.
We can sign up to be library helpers.

Ms. Lindle sees me
staring at the books.
"Do you like to read?" she asks.

I nod my head.

"Oh good," she says.
"Let me tell you about our new books."

Ms. Lindle talks and talks and talks.
I think she talks about every book in the world.
She talks about all the things you can do in the library.
She talks about authorvisits,bookbags,
bookclubs,bookdisplays,bookbingo,bookfairs,bookmarks,
booksontape,computergames,crafttables,FridayFilms,magazines,
NewReaders,WednesdayWriters,PizzaNite,
and all about the special guest who's coming in two weeks.
"A storyteller!" she says.

Before I can stop, I say,
"I tell stories too."

"You do?" Ms. Lindle smiles.
"Can you tell me one of your stories?"

I start to tell her
about Noah and the Terrible, Horrible,
Kid-Eating Dog, but then I remember
that I talk funny.
I remember the dog should be "yellow,"
not "yella."
I remember the kids making fun
of me and how my words get wedged
in my throat.

"Maybe next time," I say.
"Maybe next time," she says.

TIME

Give it time.

> You'll make friends.
> You'll fit in.

Give it time.

> It'll get better.
> It'll get easier.

I watch the clock.

> Tick tock.
> Tick tock.

When?

ALWAYS TOGETHER

When we're together,
Grandpa is slow water,

      and I'm the bubbles rising,
      I'm the minnow dart-dart-darting,
      I'm the bob-bob-bobbin.

When we're together,
Grandpa is a turtle
sunbathing on a log.

      I'm the beat of a heron's wing.
      I'm a dragonfly.

When we're together,
Grandpa is a catfish
waiting deep down low.

      But I'm a sunfish.
      I'm a wiggly tadpole.

When we're together,
we fit together just right

      like tackle and box,
      like marsh and mallow.

I'm Fish Bait.
He's Grandpa.
Best Friends Forever and fishing buds.

Chapter 4

THIRD WEEK: A FRIEND, MAYBE?

HULLO!

"For 'Dream Day,'
Allegra has brought her cockatoo
because her dream is to be a veterinarian.
Go ahead, Allegra, but before you start,
tell us about Molly Cockatoo.
How long have you had her?"

"For a year," Allegra says,
lifting Molly from the cage.

"Can she talk?"
Chloe asks.

"She can say *hello*."

"Hullo!" Molly croaks.
Everyone laughs.

"And she can say *pretty girl!*
and *peanut*. She can learn new words.
But you have to say them

over,
        and over,
                and over."

"How did you get her?"
Keith asks.

"We brought her home
from the animal shelter
where my mother works.
Molly had a broken foot."

"Can we hold her?"
someone else asks.

"Let me hold her first,"
John Royale says.
"Let me hold her!"

Allegra squinches her lips together.

"There are too many of us to pet Molly,"
Ms. Harner says. "Let's listen
to Allegra's report. She wants
to tell us about her dream,
her dream to be a veterinarian."

But everyone wants to hold Molly.
Everyone wants to feed her a peanut.

John Royale bumps Allegra's arm
and pretends to sneeze: *KAH-CHOOOOO!*

Ah-Awkkkk! Molly squawks,
batting her wings and flying up, up,
and over our heads.

"Molly!" Allegra calls,
but it's too late.
When Ms. Lindle opens the door,
with new books for our reading center,
Molly—*Ah-Awk!*—flies out into the hall.

The bell rings, and the hall
fills with noisy hurry and rumbling feet.
Through the door, we see
Ms. Lindle's book truck
and Mr. Paul's janitor cart,
but no Molly Cockatoo.

GONE!

"Oh dear," says Ms. Harner.

"I'm sorry, Allegra," Ms. Lindle says.

"I'll look for it," Mr. Paul says,
pushing his cart away.

"What if she flew outside?"
Allegra whispers.

Later, the voice of the PA says:
We have a missing bird
named Molly Cockatoo.
If you see it, please tell your teacher.
The bird belongs to Allegra Ruiz.

"I'm sorry, Allegra," I say.
"I hope you get her back."

Allegra nods.
She blinks, blinks,
blinks, as if something
is wrong with her eyes.

LIBRARY HELPER

I like to see the rainbow colors on the library shelves,
    books that are red and blue and green.

I like to feed chunks of carrots and bits of lettuce
    to the Library Gerbils, Pete and Repeat.

I like to feed the Book Guppies and the Library Goldfish
    and watch them *bubble-bubble plunk!*

I like the library when it's catfish-quiet and catfish-still,
    and also when it swims with little kids.

I like the way the books smell inky and paper-dusty,
    and the wing-swish, wing-flutter of their pages.

I like the way library books talk to me, and
    tell me stories, and make me remember
    I have stories too.

BOOK MAGIC

Sit criss-cross applesauce
under the roof of the Reading Tent.

Slip low and easy and saggy-soft
into the smoosh of a bean-bag chair.

Slowly *bump-a-beat, bump-a-beat*
in the Reading Rocker.

Perch like a frog
on a green library stool, or

find a secret spot—like I do—
in a corner, in a slant of sun,

in a quiet reading space
where you know you'll always

belong, out of sight and secret, away
from eyes that pinch and poke.

Ms. Lindle won't mind.
She says getting lost in a book

is a magic trick,
which means that I'm a wizard.

STORYTIME

"Today, our library helper is Katharen.
She has a magical book about a little boy
who puts on his wolf suit and raises a ruckus."

"*Where the Wild Things Are!*"
Nose says, and claps his hands.
"Yay!" the little kids cheer.

Ms. Lindle looks at me and nods.
I open the book carefully. At least, I try,
but it slips through my fingers and falls.

"She dropped the book," the little kids say.
"Li-berry-an! She dropped the book!"
"You're not supposed to drop the book,"
Nose whispers.

I pick the book up and remember
what Ms. Lindle taught me: P.A.S.S.

> Point to the pictures.
> Ask questions.
> Show everyone the book.
> Speak up.

"Look, here's Max in his wolf suit," I say.
"Let's say hello to Max."

"Hello!" the little kids shout.
"Hullo!" someone answers.

"Hullo!"
Over our heads, we hear a fluttering.
I stare up into the rafters.
"A bird!" the little kids shout.

"*Shhh*," Ms. Lindle hushes.
"*Shhh*, let's not frighten it.
Use your library voices."

But I don't use my library voice.
I use my feet.
I run to find Allegra.

MOLLY!

The birdcage rattles against the table.
Allegra holds up a peanut and calls again.

"Molly!"

Molly Cockatoo cocks her head
and hops along the rafter.

"The bird's not coming," Nose says.

"*Shh*," Ms. Lindle whispers.
"Everyone needs to keep quiet."

Allegra calls again
and raises her hand.
"Molly!" she says.

"*Squawk!*"
Molly answers, beating her wings
and flying from the rafter.
She flies around and around the room.
The little kids jump,
making Molly swoop higher.
"Settle down, everyone. Settle down."

Molly doesn't settle.
She flies over the computers,
over the Library Gerbils,
over the aquarium, and finally,
straight to Allegra's wrist.

"Pretty girl! Pretty girl!
Peanut! Peanut!"
Molly says.

Carefully, Allegra opens the cage door.
Carefully, she lowers Molly,
and Molly hops once, twice,
and right into the cage.

The little kids cheer.
"You put the bird in the cage!" Nose says.

Allegra looks at me.
Her face brightens
like a Fourth of July parade,
all sparkly, all shiny.

"Pretty girl! Pretty girl!
Squawkkkkkkk!"

AFTER-SCHOOL ALLEGRA

"Squawkkkk!" Nose says
and flaps his arms.

He runs to the back fence
to see Allegra.

"My name's Noah.
I live right here."

"She knows that, Nose."
I say.

"What's your name?"
Nose asks.

"Allegra."

"She's Keet-y," Nose says, pointing to me.

"Keet-y Keet-y!
Keet-y Keet-y!" Nose chants,
marching in a circle.

Allegra watches him.

"Can I see your bird?" Nose says,
flapping his arms again.

"I call him Nose because he's so nosy,
and he asks fifty zillion, trillion questions."

"Why does he call you Keet-y?"

"Because my friends say
I talk, talk, talk like a parakeet,
and I'm always telling stories."

Allegra tips her head to one side.
She rubs one shoe against the other.

"My papi called me Allie-gator
because of my front tooth."
She shows me her broken tooth.
She stares at me and waits.
But I don't say anything.

"Because my tooth
is alligator-sharp," Allegra says.

I look at her snaggly tooth.
It looks like a crooked puzzle piece.
It looks like a sharp and pointy triangle.

"My grandpa saw an alligator once," I say.
"It snatched a bird right out of the water.
He said alligators are quick and strong.
We like alligators."

Allie-gator smiles.

I smile back.

Nose squawks.

"I collect feathers," Allie-gator says.

"I collect hats and cups," I say.

Allie-gator smiles again.
I like her crooked smile.

"Can you cartwheel?"
Allegra asks.

I shake my head.

"I'll teach you," and she throws her hands
against the ground and pushes herself into a cartwheel.

"Teach me, too!" Nose says.
"Teach me to wheel, too!
Help me, Keet!
Help me, Allie-gator!"

LIBRARY FISH

Keet: Grandpa, I signed up to be a library helper.
             I get to go to the library during recess,
             and I get to take care of the library fish.

Grandpa: Fishing in the library, Fish Bait?
             Well, isn't that something.

Keet: No! No, Grandpa, we can't fish in the library.
             I didn't say *fishing*. I said *fish*.

Grandpa: What kind of fish can you catch in your library?
             I'll bring my fishing pole and we can try it out.

Keet: Grandpa!

SATURDAY:
FISHING LESSON #4

Our fishing lines reel out.
The sun wheels overhead.

We sit and wait for a nibble,
a bite, a tug on the line.

Quiet time, inside-my-head time,
listening time, looking out—

a leaf spins,

                a frog leaps,

tiny shells sink in the mud,

                a great blue heron
pinches a fish with its beak.

      "Look,"

the water murmurs.

                The wind whispers,

"Look, again."

Chapter 5

FOURTH WEEK: WIGGLE WORMS AND SAND PLUMS

SETTLING IN #2

"Looks like you're settling in," Mama says.

Am I?
I have a friend, now.
I get to fish with Grandpa.
I get to help in the library.
But what happened to the girl I used to be?

Mama looks around my room and smiles.
She studies the cups on my shelf.

The flowery teacup that belonged to Grandma.
The cup with my name on it that Daddy found in Kansas City.
The plastic cup with pink poodles that Nose gave me for my
    birthday.
The green cup with a goldfish hidden inside.
And my favorite cup, the cup Mama gave me,
        cracked and broken like a puzzle
        because I dropped it.

Carefully, Mama lifts the broken cup from the shelf.

"Do you remember your story, Keet?"
"Yes," I say. I used to tell the story
to anyone who looked at my cup collection.

The Cup of Midnight Blue

Once I had a beautiful porcelain cup.
The cup was midnight blue, ink blue,
with four gold legs and a tiny picture
of the sea painted on each side.
It was thin and delicate and very old.
Mama gave it to me.

It was my favorite cup.
I used it for my chocolate milk.
I used it for pineapple juice,
and I used it for chamomile tea.

But one day,
while I sip-sip-sipped,
my fingers slipped,
and the cup tipped, toppled, tumbled
down, and broke into pieces.
I felt like purple berry juice spilled in a puddle.
Mama picked the pieces up,
but she didn't throw them away.
Instead she found a special glue
and glued the cup together
piece by piece by piece.
Then she brought it back to me.

"Isn't it pretty, Keet?"

"No," I said.

"But Keet, just because your cup has cracks,
or isn't perfect like it used to be,
doesn't mean it can't be beautiful."

I didn't want to believe her.
"It still won't hold anything," I said.

"No, not juice, not milk, not tea," Mama said,
"but maybe a broken cup can hold other things."

I didn't think so. "I want another cup," I said.
"I wish it wasn't broken." Wish, wishes,
wishing, *I thought. "What if*
this were a wishing cup? I could fill it
with wishes. That's what I'll do.
It will be the best cup of all."

It's our favorite story, but the words won't come.
I can't tell it. I feel Mama watching me.
"I think I'll make a wish," she says.
"I wish that my parakeet knew how much
I love her and that once she settles in
she'll tell me stories again. That's my wish,
Keet-Keet." She sets the cup back on the shelf.

It is still my favorite cup.
It is still beautiful.

I close my eyes and think
about school and the Keet who used
to talk and tell stories. I make a wish
and drop it deep inside the midnight cup.

TIRED

I hear a deep humming noise
and then a slamming car door.
Daddy's home! Daddy's home!
Nose and I run to the door.
Mama says, "Slow down.
Don't knock him over."

I grab Daddy around the waist,
and Nose hugs his knees.

Daddy! Daddy! Daddy!

Daddy drives now for a delivery company.
He drives a big truck up and down
the highway and in and out of town.

Sometimes, he has to drive so far away
that we don't see him for days.
Sometimes, he comes home late at night
tired, tired, and goes to bed.
But sometimes, when it's not so late,
he says, "Tell me a story, Keet,"
and I curl up on his lap. I squeeze close.

I want to tell him the story about
the time we found the sand plums.
I want to, but I don't. I can't be
the story-talking, story-making girl,
telling stories about the things I did
or making stories up.

"I . . . I don't have a story, Daddy."
He looks at me.
     He doesn't tease.
          He doesn't ask why.
He just pulls me closer and strokes
my head like he does when I'm sick,
his fingers against my braids, trying
to stroke the troubles away.

KEET'S STORY ABOUT
THE SAND PLUMS

"Stop the car!"

Mama sees a grove of sand plums,
ripe plums, round plums,
sand plums for jelly.

Daddy and me,
Nose, and Mama
climb out of the car
and walk through
a grassy ditch
and up a sloping bank.

A grasshopper flutters
and lands on my sock.
I brush it away.
Another grasshopper lands in my hair
and I squeal.

At the top of the slope,
the air around the sand plums
is gnatty and buzzy.
Sunlight spills on our heads
as if we are plums too.

Mama plucks the sand plums
from the twiggy branches.
She hands them to us,
orange-red, and plump, and sun-warm.
If we squeeze too hard, the plums
make our fingers licky with juice.

Mama folds the bottom
of her dress to make a basket
and fills it with ripe sand plums.

She gives me a plum.
I hold it in my hand:
                          a little sun.
I bite it and feel sunshine
deep down in my stomach.

DEEP INSIDE

This side, that side,
inside, outside,
in the center,
in the middle,
in the midst,
in the muddle of me,

there's a box—
a heart box
a dream box
a secrets box
with lots of locks.

And only Mama
only Daddy
only Grandpa
only Noah
have a key.

But maybe
I will give one key more,
to Allie-gator,
if she'll give me a key

to the box
the heart box
the thoughts box
the this-is-what-I-feel box
the box with locks
in the center,
in the midst,
in the middle-middle
muddle of her.

ALLIE-GATOR SAYS

I like her.
I like her flippy floppy braids.
I like the way she makes me laugh.
I like the funny way she talks.
I like when she tells me stories about her grandpa.
I like when she tells me stories about Alabama,
    where she used to live.
I like when she talks about her grandma,
    who's not alive anymore.
I like that she likes stars, ice cream, bicycles,
    monkey bars, sidewalk chalk, cups,
    chocolate chip cookies, funny socks, hats,
    jumping rope, and
    peanutbutterdillpickle sandwiches.
I like when she finds feathers to add to my collection.
I like that she said my house was nice, even
    though it's not as nice as hers.
I like the way she laughed and laughed and laughed
    when Molly Cockatoo said *Hullo!*
    What cha doing? Hullo! What cha doing?
I like that she doesn't make fun of my crooked
    snaggletooth, my pointy tooth, my chipped tooth,
    my cracked and jagged puzzle-tooth
    or my alligator smile.
I like the Me I see in her deep-water eyes.

KEET SAYS

I like her.
I like going to her house.
I like climbing trees and scraping our knees.
I like that she likes spaghetti and big fat meatballs.
I like when she lets me taste *horchata,* her mother's cinnamon
    rice milk.
I like when she tells me about her abuela, her grandma,
    who lives with her.
I like that she likes my daddy because her daddy's
    not alive anymore, which makes me sad.
I like that she likes birds, chocolate cake, drawing, swings,
    big boxes of crayons, rocking chairs, bracelets, the color
    blue, blowing bubbles, firecrackers, and volleyball.
I like that she draws and makes all kinds of things with paper,
    even paper beads.
I like when she lets me hold Molly Cockatoo
    and feed her grapes.
I like when she comes to my house and talks to my mother.
I like when Nose asks her 100 billion questions about birds
    and she answers every one.
I like that she doesn't like math.
I like that she has a goldfinch feather, robin feather, hawk
    feather, blue jay feather, wren feather, chicken feather,
    goose feather, and even a peacock feather.
I like that *f-r-i-e-n-d* is a hard word to spell,
but Allegra spells it: K-a-t-h-a-r-e-n.

YOU CAN'T SPELL IT, ALLIE-GATOR

Keet: I'll make you a bet, Allie-gator.

Allie-gator: You won't win.

Keet: Yes, I will. I found a really hard word this time.

Allie-gator: If I can spell it, I get a story
                 like you used to tell your Alabama friends.

Keet: If I win, I get to feed Molly a bag of peanuts,
                 hold her for as long as I want to,
                 and teach her to say my name.

Allie-gator: Uh-uh, just a bag of peanuts.

Keet: All right, a *big* bag of peanuts. But
                 you have to spell *preposterous*.

Allie-gator: You're using your Alabama voice
                 to make it harder.

Keet: Yup!

KEET'S SCARY STORY FOR ALLIE-GATOR

Late one night,
I watched
a really, really, super scary
ghost story on TV.

I was all by myself,
in the basement,
eating popcorn,
and watching
the lady ghost
who lived in an old house
and oozed through the door
and scared everyone.
Then I went upstairs
to get another glass
of apple-orange juice
with lots of ice.

The lights were low,
and only the spooky-ghosty
blue light
from the TV
was shining.

I put my foot on the first step
to go up the stairs.

Eeeechhhhh.

Was that noise behind me?

I turned around.
All I saw
was the dark, dark
basement
with the blue-ghosty
light from the TV.

I took a step
and another step.

    Eeechhhh.

I pushed my foot on top of the step:
no sound.

I pushed my foot really hard
on the step: no sound.

I looked behind me
in the dark, dark basement.
I looked at the blue and spooky,
blue and ghosty light
from the TV.

I took a step
and then another step

    Eechhhhh.

Something was behind me.
I knew it!

Something was following me.
I just knew it!

It was the ghost woman
from the TV.
I knew it, just knew it!

I raised my foot to get ready to run.
I raised my leg to race up the stairs.
I took a step. Then I heard it,
and then I knew!

Eechhhhhh.

My knee!
My knee creaked.
My knee squeaked like a rusty door!
I had a spooky-ghosty knee:

Eechhhhhh.

SLEEPOVER

1. Pajamas on and fuzzy slippers,
2. Chocolate cookies, chocolate milk,
3. Homework finished,
4. (Even math),
5. Fingernail polish for twenty toes,
6. A rap song, a TV show,
7. Drawing pictures,
8. Potato stamps,
9. Laugh so hard your stomach cramps,
10. Play Monopoly,
11. Play Go Fish,
12. Baby brother—such a nuisance!
13. Blowing bubbles,
14. Milk and cookies,
15. Milk mustache,
16. Putting on my funny hats,
17. Practice handstands on the mats,
18. Try on lipstick,
19. Try on rings,
20. What if we had magic wings?
21. More cookies, more milk,
22. Pink ice cream and pillow fight,
23. Laughter rising like a kite,
24. Mama turns out all the lights,
25. Girl giggles: *ark! ark!*
26. Telling stories in the dark,
27. Shadow fingers on the wall,
28. Daddy's warning, our last call,

29. Little brother, little sneak
squeezing in beneath our sheet.

Good night, Allie-gator.
Good night, Keet.
Good night, Nose.
Now go to sleep!

LOUD

Too loud
the alarm clock.

Too loud
the sun.

Too loud
Mama calling,

"Get up,
everyone."

Too loud
the words,
"Keet, it's time
for school."

Too loud
my yawn.

Too loud.
Too loud.

Where has
nighttime gone?

HALLWAY ELEPHANTS

After the bell, we come rumbling,
racing, and stomping down the hall,

herding through the doorways,
trumpeting our calls,
romping with giggles, with gossip,
and now and then a shout,
pushing and tumbling everyone all about.

The walls bounce and echo
with every kind of loud:
locker slams, book whams,
lunchbox flops and bags that pop,
heels sliding to a stop,
cell phones ringing, singers singing.

Until the teacher claps and shouts,
"Quiet, quiet, quiet!"
This isn't the Serengeti.
This isn't a circus tent.
But not a one of us seems
to know what the teacher meant.

PENCIL SONG

When the room is quiet,
if I press my ear
to my desk,
I hear my pencil
slide, scrape, stutter.

I can hear
the pencil humming
and rolling my words
along,

slipping and pushing
its lead like the tongue
of a new kid at school

saying words
with difficult letters,
practicing the sounds
over and over
trying to get them right,
to make them slip
from the lip, smooth and swift,
like everybody else.

KEET'S SCIENCE EXPERIMENT:
WORM WATCH

1. Gently place the worm's body on the wax paper in the tray.
   Observe the worm's movements.

Poor worm

twist

thrash

wiggle

thump

Poor, poor worm

2. Use the hand lens to study the worm. Describe its body.

Long, pencil-thin, a whip of skin, a soft twisty-
twig, a rubber band stretching,
reaching, shrinking. Segmented rings on a rubbery
tube, wiry hairs, pointy
at the end, plump in the middle, a tiny vacuum
cleaner hose.

3. Sprinkle a layer of soil on top of the wax paper. Place the
worm on the soil. Observe the worm's movements.

I glide.
I stretch. I slide. How easily
I grip the dirt with my spiky hairs. How easily
I plow and push and mine. How easily I move
from here to there.

4. What conclusions can you reach from your experiment?

Out-of-place
>Everything is hard,

Out-of-place
>A worm finds it hard to be a worm.

Out-of-place
>Does a worm feel wormy,
>or only small and lost?

ALLEGRA'S SCIENCE EXPERIMENT:
WORM WATCH

1. Gently place the worm's body on the wax paper in the tray.
    Observe the worm's movements.

    (Pencil drawing:
    A line.)

2. Use the hand lens to study the worm. Describe its body.

    tube, cylinder, segments,
    a long triangle head.

3. Sprinkle a layer of soil on top of the wax paper. Place the
    worm on the soil. Observe the worm's movements.

    (Pencil drawing:
    A worm in a tunnel beneath the dirt.
    The grass growing overhead—safe.)

4. What conclusions can you reach from your experiment?

    A line,
    a squiggly line, a wiggly line,
    a straight line.

    Letters are made with lines.
    Are words worms?

Chapter 6

FIFTH WEEK: FISHING FOR WORDS

IN LINE

In line
march march march
by the wall
hands to self
march march march
to the library to the gym
to the lunchroom back again
march march march
at the fountain—line up
at the door—line up
straight backs
eyes ahead
knees up
knees down
march march march
the teacher watches with ruler eyes
our school parade
our school brigade
students marching marching
marching in line
down the hall
around the corner
through the doors
and then outside
running
   jumping
hopping
   skipping
leaping
   spinning
in loops

in groups
and alley-oops
under the hoops
monkey-swinging on monkey bars
somersaults cartwheels
circles and squares
but no lines

ALL THE TALKIN' I'VE HEARD

"If everyone can sit in a semi-circle,
I'll introduce our storyteller, Doug McVicker."

The storyteller is a giant.
He has a guitar,
and his voice rumbles and rolls
like rocks tumbling down a mountain.
Doug McVicker says he comes from Tennessee.
He says he comes from Appalachia.

"You sound funny," John Royale says.

Doug McVicker just laughs.
"Sound like good ol' Tennessee," he says.
"My voice is a map of all the places I've been
and all the talkin' I've heard.
My stories sound that way too."

Then Doug McVicker tells us his stories.

> We laugh.
> We shout.
> We sing.
> We squeal.

Our eyes beam like flashlights
and pictures flash inside our heads.

He tells us that if we know someone's story,
then we know who they are,
and knowing someone's story—"Well,"
Doug McVicker says,
in his good ol' Tennessee voice,
"knowing someone's story is one way
to put an end to a lot of trouble in the world.

"For my next story, I need a volunteer.
I need someone to help me tell the story."

I duck my head.
I try to make myself invisible.
But Allie-gator squints her eyes at me.
You tell stories, her eyes say.
You tell good stories.
And then,
not too high,
not too fast,
but slowly, slowly,
I raise my hand.

Everyone looks at me.
Ms. Lindle smiles.
John Royale smirks.
(He's always smirking.)

The storyteller teaches me what to say.
He shows me what to do.
We tell the story together.
He tells it, really.
I just do the in-between parts.

Everybody listens.
Everybody leans in and scooches close.
Everybody laughs when I say my part.
They don't laugh at me
or the way I say the words.
They laugh at the story.
Even Allie-gator smiles (well, almost).
Even John Royale pays attention.

Clap! Clap! Clappity!
Hooting and rooting!

"Take a bow," Doug McVicker says.
"You're a good storyteller."

Good, he said that I was good.
G-o-o-d with two O's
round as sand plums,
round like two shining suns,
round like eggs waiting to hatch.

MAYBE ME

I think about the storyteller
and telling stories.

The way all the kids listened.

The way everyone clapped.

It didn't matter that they thought
he had a funny voice.

I have an Alabama voice.
I sound like Mama-Daddy-Grandpa-
Grandma-Brother,
all my uncle-aunties
and all my hundred-hundred cousins.
I sound like all the talking I've heard,
and all the singing,
and all the stories, too.

SPLASH!

Maybe my voice
is hiding
deep down inside

like a catfish.
Maybe it's listening,

waiting to rise,
to splash, to leap
into the air
like a rainbow.

Maybe it's waiting
for the right bait.

FISHING LESSON #5

Slippery, slippery,
wide as my hand.
I feel its weight, feel the slick
of its smooth scales. I see
a flat and shiny eye staring back.
Sharp fins flare,
sharp spines slash.
Scaled, mailed,
it flaps and claps its tail.

It does not like the air.
It does not like the light.
It does not like my hand's rough drought.

Grandpa pries the hook from its lip.
I stare into its eye. It stares at me.

"What do you think, Fish Bait?"

I lower the fish carefully into the water.
The fish floats, stunned and slow,
but then—*plonk!* It swims away.

Rings of water where it used to be,
rings spreading out, out, out.

SATURDAY:
FISHING LESSON #6

Out, out, out, I throw my fishing line out, out, out across the

muddy water to plunge—*splish-splash*—down into the slow,

slow slide, the muddy glide and ooze, letting my line sink

and settle, long sun-struck string, and bob-bob-bobbin' in the

mud-mirrored waters, to drift and drift and duck—dip, dip,

dip—to the shy nib-nibbling of a fish or maybe the soft

ba-bump, ba-bump beating of my heart.

FISHING LESSON #7

Bait your hook with patience,
if you want to catch a fish.

Bait your hook with be still,
be quiet, be slow.

Bait your hook with mosquito-buzzing,
with dragonfly-darts and frog-plops.

Bait your hook with shadows,
with a crow's *awk-awk* and with sunlight.

Bait your hook with just enough wind
to cool the heat but not too much.

Bait your hook with your grandpa's
steady breath and the way he smiles at you.

But mostly, bait your hook with listening, with waiting,
with low waves bumping against the bank.

Chapter 7

SIXTH WEEK: THE NEW GRANDPA

AN ORDINARY DAY

It seemed like an ordinary day.
I sat at my desk practicing my spelling words,
erasing my math, reading about reptiles.

It seemed like an ordinary day.
But then the School Office called my teacher.
My teacher looked at me.

It seemed like an ordinary day.
"Katharen, please gather up your things.
You need to go to the office."

It seemed like an ordinary day.
But Mama was in the office
and Nose too
with his backpack and his book
about kangaroos. He likes animals,
my little brother. He likes worms
and bugs. I watch him
kick-kicking at the rug.

It seemed like an ordinary day.
But then Mama said,
"We need to go, Katharen,
something bad has happened."

Something bad when I was at school.
Something bad when I was spelling *Octapuses* or *Octopie*.
Something bad when I divided 5,408 by 52.
Something bad when Allie-gator passed me a note:
"You want to come over after school?"

It seemed like an ordinary day.
But it wasn't.

HOSPITAL RAIN

Words fall
like rain
      drops,
heavy, gray words.

I hear *stroke, minor.*
I hear *should recover.*
I hear *depression possible.*
I hear *physical therapy.*
I hear Grandpa's name.

I hear *wait and see.*
I hear Mama crying
and Daddy saying,
"It'll be all right."

Something bad has happened.

I sit next to Nose,
and he snuggles against me.

I feel drops of rain falling
from my eyes, big fat heavy
gray drops of rain.

THE NEW GRANDPA

His eyes are dark rainy days.
Mama says he'll stay with us
until he gets better, until
he gets stronger. I tiptoe
by his door. I don't want to go in.

"It's okay, Keet.
You can talk to him," Mama says.

I go in, but I don't see *my* Grandpa.
I see a new Grandpa.

He is thin and wrinkle-faced.
He is sad and quiet.

"Daddy, look," Mama says. "Keet is here.
Do you want to say hello to her?"

The New Grandpa looks at me.
But he doesn't say anything.
He just looks old.
His lips tremble, and his hands tremble.
His eyes are dark rainy days.

KEET

GRANDPA

I want my old grandpa,

but I'm no use to anyone
now. I'm not

the grandpa who laughed

the strong man. The man
who raised a family.

and fished and listened.

And scrambled for a living.
Who did his best.

I love you, I try to say,

I try to say *You're all I have*,
but

words are slippery fish;

words are deep water. I'm
sinking:

inside I'm a dark river.

Got an anchor in my heart,
too heavy to lift.

NO WORDS

Allie-Gator:

Keet came to school today.
But she didn't talk to me.
I showed her my new collage.
I gave her my cookie at lunchtime.
"I hope your grandpa gets better," I said.
But she didn't say anything.
I almost said, "Can you come over?"
I almost said, "Do you feel bad?"
Almost, but my words were turtle-slow.

Keet:

Ms. Harner said, "We missed you, Katharen."
The kids looked at me funny.
I heard them whispering.
Allie-Gator showed me her new collage.
She gave me her cookie at lunchtime.
She said she was sorry about Grandpa.
Allie-Gator likes Grandpa.
I almost said, "Do you want to come over?"
I almost said, "How's Molly Cockatoo?"
Almost, but my words were turtle-slow.

ALLIE-GATOR'S WISH

I want my friend Keet-Keet back.
The talking girl, the story girl.
But I'll try to be patient. I'll try to listen,
until her sad days, her bad days, go away.

Talking girl, story girl.
Can't you laugh again with me?
Until the sad times, the bad times, go away?
We're girl glue: me + you.

Can't you laugh again with me?
I'm Allie-gator, I'm your friend.
We're girl glue: me + you.
"Give her time," Abuela says.

I'm Allie-gator, I'm your friend.
Tell me a story, talk to me.
"*Darle tiempo*," Abuela says.
Won't you laugh, Keet-Keet?

I'll keep asking for your stories.
I'll try to be patient. I'll try to listen.
I'm Allie-gator and you're *mi amiga*.
I want Keet-Keet back, *por favor*.

KEET'S WISH

I want my Old Grandpa back.
Keep your line tight, Keet.
I won't give up. I'll tell him stories.
I'll make the sad go away.

Keep your line tight, Keet.
Grandpa, can you talk to me?
I'll make the sad go away.
Guess what I did, Grandpa?

Grandpa, can you talk to me?
I'll listen with my inside ear.
Guess what I did, Grandpa?
"Give him time," Mama says.

I'll listen with my inside ear.
Don't cry, Grandpa, I love you.
"Give him time," Mama says.
I hold Grandpa's hand. I kiss his cheek.

I'll use talking and stories for bait.
I won't give up. I'll tell him stories.
I'll talk and talk his sad away.
I want my Old Grandpa back.

RAINY DAYS

Mama hugs me tight.
"It'll be all right, Keet.
It'll be all right."

"Is he going to get better?"

"He's feeling down, Keet,
and his body's weak. But
he's doing his physical therapy
and he'll get better. You'll see.
We just have to keep his spirits up."

"Does he still love us?"

"Of course Grandpa loves us!
Especially you and Noah."

"How do you know?"

"You're his Fish Bait, Keet,
the girl who Grandpa says
can talk his ears all the way to Texas
and have them back in time for supper.
The girl who makes him laugh.
The girl who takes him fishing.

"He told me once
that his heart was an old tackle box
and that you were the best thing in it."

MOONLIGHT

Daddy does his best to get home
before I go to bed. But sometimes
he's late and I fall asleep.
Daddy's late tonight, but when he
gets home, he tiptoes into my room
and whispers in my ear.

I slip on my slippers,
and Daddy picks me up
in my pajamas and swoops me
high above his head
to perch on his shoulders.

Quietly, Daddy steps
out of the house.
Quietly, he shuts the door,
and we walk through the ink-black,
skillet-black, down-in-a-deep-
deep-hole-black night
to the rickety picnic table
where he sits me down to look
up into the far, far away,
up into the starry polka-dotty night.

We look, like we used to,
for our shiny friends:

the Big Dipper,
Orion's Belt, and
the Little Dipper,
and there in its highest seat,
the Moon Milk Pie.
That's what I called it
when I was little,
and that's what Daddy
calls it now.

"Look how bright it is tonight, Keet.
Look how bright."

I fold my hands into a cup
and let the moonlight spill in.
I tip it full into Daddy's hands,
and he raises it to his lips
to sip, sip, sip,
and then he does the same for me.

"*Mmmm*," I say,
"nothing like Moon Milk,"
just like I used to do.

Daddy smiles,
and Moon Milk spills
over us
until we shine.

A SHINY SHEET OF PAPER

Grandpa doesn't say anything,
but he watches carefully.
He watches closely as Allie-gator
draws a shiny sheet of orange paper
from her pocket. Then Allie-gator
sits beside Grandpa's bed
and smoothes the paper flat.
She folds it this way and folds
it that way. She creases the lines
ruler-straight and knife-edge sharp.
And then she unfolds the paper.
A fish! A shiny orange goldfish!

Allie-gator sets the fish on Grandpa's windowsill.
I watch Grandpa's eyes follow Allie-gator.
I watch him looking at the fish.
I watch him studying me
like my Old Grandpa did, but then
he closes his eyes and creases them tight
and seals my Old Grandpa   away.

SAD

Sad comes. It will not go away.
It sits in the bathtub
and makes the water cold.

It follows me to breakfast
and wants runny eggs and soggy toast.

It tries to do my homework,
especially math.
It thinks the answer is always zero.

Sad puts on my clothes,
when I don't want it to.
Sad wants to wear my shoes
and do whatever I do.

I look in the mirror and I see Sad
staring at me.
I stick my tongue out at it.
It sticks its tongue out too.
Go away, Sad, I say. Go far away.

It opens its mouth,
but nothing comes out.
There are no words, and
no word is right.

Sad makes it hard to answer
when Mama asks,
"What's the matter, Honey?
Tell me what you want."

CATCHING GRANDPA

I want to find my Old Grandpa.
I think he's hiding inside this New Grandpa.

I think he's deep-down low like
an old catfish. But I know he hears me.
I know he does.

I'm going to tell him stories.
I'll use Grandpa's fishing lessons.

"Keep your line tight,"
Grandpa used to say.

"If one bait doesn't work, try another,"
Grandpa used to say.

"Pull your line a little and let go a little,"
Grandpa used to say.

"You've got to be patient if you want
to catch a fish,"
Grandpa used to say.

I'll catch you, Grandpafish,
that's what I say.

Dive, deep, deep,

    and I'll follow.

Twist and turn,

      and I'll hold tight.

Try to draw yourself away,

      and I'll make my stories into a net
      and wrap them snug around you.

KEET'S STORY FOR GRANDPA
ABOUT THE GREAT BIG ROCKET

Ms. Harner tells us to write a fable,
a story with a lesson. I think and I think,
until at last a fable swims into my head.
I call it, "The Fable of Jack's Rocket."

Once there was a boy named Jack
who liked to draw
who had an assignment to draw a rocket.

Lightning-quick, Jack drew
a long skinny rectangle
with a triangle on top.
Jack was pleased with his rocket.
Jack was the first one in his class to finish.

Jack carried his rocket
to the front of the room
to place it on the teacher's desk,
just like the teacher said.

Or at least
he started to,
but then he saw
another kid's rocket.

The other rocket was bigger.
It had wide windows
with people looking out.

Jack didn't turn his rocket in.
He sat back down and drew
a brand-new rocket.
His new rocket was much bigger.
It had wide windows.
It had people looking out.
Jack was pleased.

He carried his new rocket
to the front of the room
to put on the teacher's desk.

Or at least
he started to—
but then he saw
another kid's rocket.

It had curlicues of smoke
and jets of fire.
It flew through space
with blue and purple stars.
The other rocket was better
than Jack's rocket.

So Jack sat down
and started over.
He drew an even larger rocket
with smoke and curlicues,
and jets of fire, and windows
with people looking out,
and a sky filled with stars,
and a big, wide yellow moon.
Jack was pleased.

He carried his new rocket
to the front of the room
to put on the teacher's desk,
just like the teacher said.

At least—
Jack started to,
but then he saw another kid's rocket.
It had an astronaut
floating from a curly rope
and a space alien with an antenna.
The other kid's rocket
was better than Jack's rocket.

So Jack sat down
and started over.
He drew and he drew
until there was nothing left of Jack
but his crayon moving around
and around, drawing rockets
and rockets and rockets
over and over and over . . .

KEET'S STORY FOR GRANDPA
ABOUT THE TERRIBLE, HORRIBLE,
KID-EATING DOG

Once Nose and I
walked to the store.
It was an old store,
a neighborhood store,
with a screen door
that whacked and slammed.
It smelled like coffee
and had rows of shelves,
and a cooler
with popsicles and ice cream,
and boxes of candy,
and gumballs
for a quarter.

We had six quarters
and twenty-five pennies.
We walked
past the houses,
past the fences,
past the mailboxes,
past our new school,
until
we reached
the yellow-and-brown
house with the low gate.

Then I went tip-
toe, tiptoe along the sidewalk,
going by the house
tiptoe quiet and tiptoe quick.
But Nose went
CLOP clop, CLOP clop,
because he had on Daddy's shoes.

We had almost
made it to the next house,
when across the yard
of the yellow-and-brown house,
and through its low gate,
ran
the scariest
        dog
in the whole wide world,

a big-eyed, pointy-eared,
sharp-toothed, snotty-nosed Chihuahua,
                        and it barked,
            and barked,
and BARKED
at Nose and me.

Then it chased us!

I was scared. I ran.
Nose was scared.
He ran, or tried to.
CLOP CLOP, CLOP CLOP.
He started to cry
and call my name,

but I was too scared.
I ran fast for the store,
for the squeaky screen door
that would whack
and slam behind me.

I ran faster than Nose.
The terrible Chihuahua was right behind him.

CLOP! CLOP! CLOP! CLOP!

BARK! BARK! BARK! BARK!

Then the old man
who lived in the yellow-and-brown house
gave a sharp whistle.

The dog stopped.

He turned and trotted
back to his yard
like a little yellow king,
a horrible monster dog,
a kid catcher.

Nose cried
for a long time.
I felt bad.
I didn't save him.
I wasn't a superhero or a wizard.
I didn't have a magic cape.

So I let him have five quarters
and all the pennies.
I took the last quarter
and bought a gumball.
He got a popsicle and ate it
all by himself,
and he didn't give me any.

ANY FOR ME?

I tell Grandpa a story every day.
I tell him:

"How I Walk Noah to School," and
"How I Made Cornbread Soup with Mama," and
"The Great Cream-Puff Disaster," and
"Earthworms Everywhere," and
"Allie-Gator Can Spell Anything."

I tell all kinds of stories, new ones
and old ones. Grandpa listens to every one.
Sometimes, he falls asleep, but he always
wakes up and listens again. Once,
when I came home, he was sitting
up in bed waiting for me.

Today, I tell him about making
stamps in art class and eating
three slices of pizza for lunch.
Grandpa's lips wobble into a smile,
and he says, in a slurry voice,

"Did you save any for me?
Fisssh Bait?"

When I look at his face,
I can see my Old Grandpa.
I can see two guppy-sized girls
in his eyes, and they look just like me.

Chapter 8

SEVENTH WEEK: SAY SOMETHING, KEET!

"DREAM DAY"

"Katharen," Ms. Harner calls.
Every eye turns to me.
"We're looking forward
to hearing your report
for 'Dream Day.'
It will be your turn next week."

Me? My turn? How can that be?

John Royale will laugh.
Chloe will sneer.
Everyone will say I sound funny,
that my words hurt their ears.

Maybe I'll be sick.
Maybe I'll stay home.
Maybe I'll catch a boat to Timbuktu or Rome.

Allie-gator gives me a note:
"You'll be MAGNIFICENT. You'll see."

NOSY POSY

Allie-gator comes over to see me after school.
But sometimes she comes to see Nose.

Nosy Nose has a secret.
He's doing something with Allie-gator. What?

Mama keeps me busy in the house
so that I don't find out.

"What are they up to?" I say. "What are they doing?"

"Who's the nosy one now?" Mama laughs.

I don't know. But I know
they're up to something fishy.

"Nosy posy," Mama says.
"Keet's a nosy posy."

FISH COUNT

Nose likes to count the fish
on Grandpa's windowsill,
different sizes, different shapes.
Allie-gator made them all.
When she comes over after school,
Grandpa sits up a little higher in bed.
Is he feeling better? Today, he looks
at something on his bedside table,
and then he looks at Allie-gator,
and then he looks at me.

Allie-gator doesn't hesitate.
She picks up the gum wrapper,
and folds triangle-y angles
into a teeny-tiny, itty-
bitty gum-wrapper goldfish.

Allie-gator sets the fish
on the windowsill.
Grandpa looks at her,
and then he looks at me.
His mouth trembles a little
and then he smiles, a small smile.
"That-s-sahh keeper!" he says.

SWIMMING AWAY

Allie-gator keeps telling silly fish jokes.

"Keet, what did the catfish say to the librarian?
     Got any fish tales?"

"Keet, why did the catfish skip school?
     It was playing fish hooky."

"Keet, why don't they serve catfish in the school cafeteria?
     The catfish and hotdogs always fight."

I want to smile because
     I've found a friend,
     because Grandpa's getting better and talking a little
       more,
     because Mama's singing to herself like she used to do,
     because Nose is still my silly baby brother.

I want to smile, I try to,
but then I remember
"Dream Day."

I have stories now for Allegra,
and stories for Grandpa,
but at school—

my stories snarl like fishing lines,
my talking catches mean-kid looks,
my words slip and swim away,
and the storyfish sinks deep inside.

CAN

"Keep trying, Keet,
you can do anything
you put your mind to,"
my grandma used to say.

But I have to give
a "Dream Day" talk,
and I don't say the words the way
the other kids say them.

I think about the storyteller,
who made it seem so easy. But it isn't easy.

Inside my head, I hear Mama say,
"You can do it, Keet."

I remember Allie-gator's note.
"You'll be MAGNIFICENT. You'll see."

I imagine Nose singing over and over,
"Keet-y can. Keety-can."

I think about Grandpa's fishing lesson.
"Plant your feet, Keet, and pull, pull, pull."

I think of Daddy tugging my braids,
looking me in the eye, and giving me a wink.
Daddy always thinks I can do it.

But what if I don't think,
really don't think I can?

GENIE

"Grandpa," I whisper. "I don't think I can do it."
But Grandpa is sound asleep.
He doesn't hear me.
He doesn't know
that I really, really need him.

I whisper, "Don't let the fishes bite,"
like he used to say.
But Grandpa is fast asleep.

I don't know what to do.
I hold his hand and rub it
like I'm making wishes on a genie lamp.

Grandpa

Grandpa

Grandpa

WHAT WILL I SAY?

I repeat the words over and over:
You can do it. You can do it.
But—I can't. I know I can't.

They'll say I say things wrong.
They'll look at me
and think I don't belong.

I try to remember what the storyteller said.
I try to remember Grandpa's fishing lessons.
I try—but in my head
I see eyes like measuring tape.
I see faces like sour grapefruits.
I hear voices chanting:
Katharen Walker, funny talker.

Don't look! Don't listen to them,
to the kids who say you can't do it.

You can do it, Keet-Keet.
You can do it, Keet.
You can do it, Katharen!

But what will I tell them
for "Dream Day"?
What can I talk about?
What can I say?
Do I have a dream today?

MY KNEES ARE KNOCKING

My hands are grasshoppers
my heart is a kangaroo
my lungs are too small
my throat is a desert
my tongue . . .

                where's my tongue?

CATCHING A STORYFISH

"If you're going to catch a fish,
you can't be afraid of the water,"
Grandpa used to say.

"You got to be quiet and still."

I let myself get quiet.
I stand very still.
I feel my heart skipping rope.

I remember the storyteller's words.
My voice is all the places I've been
and all the stories I've heard.

It's Grandpa, Grandma, Mama, Daddy,
and Nose. It's my uncles, aunties,
and my hundred-hundred cousins.

I open my mouth
and let the words come.

I tell them about Grandpa.

I tell them how to find
the best fishing holes,
and the best bait.

I tell them Grandpa's recipes
for scaring away mosquitoes.

I tell them about turtles
and water striders and great blue herons
and minnows, sunfish,
bass, and carp with diamond-shiny scales.

I tell them about cleaning fish,
and fishing poles as tall as a house,
and all the different kinds of bait:
red wigglers, night crawlers,
crickets, hoppers, stinky dough balls,
chicken livers, and even marshmallows.

I tell them about deep water
and shallow water, and water rings
beating against the shore.

I tell them how you have to stay quiet
and still and not move, not even
when you have an itch.

I tell them about keeping catfish-quiet
and not wiggling anything, not even your nose.

I tell them my dream,
to go fishing with Grandpa again,
and how we will catch Ol' Muddy Joe,
and Grandpa and I will stay together, forever forever.

I tell them about the storyfish
that Grandpa says I have inside.
And how sometimes a story
swims through my heart
and leaps up all silvery
and rainbow-bright. I tell them
I dream of catching my storyfish
and telling a really good story
that makes my grandpa smile again.

I lift things from my heart box
one by one to show them.

I talk for a long time.

But no one says a word,
not even Ms. Harner,
not even Ms. Lindle,
who comes to deliver books
and then sits down to listen.
The room is quiet.
Every face is still.
Everyone stares,
their eyes like dark windows.
Their mouths are like doors
to scary houses, some sealed,
some open. Even Allegra
has a strange look.
I feel ice cubes in my head.
I feel fishhooks. I feel
tangly nets. I feel mosquitoes buzzing
and angry bees. I don't ask
permission. I don't ask for a pass.
I don't wait for Ms. Harner
to dismiss me from class.
I jump and run out the door.
"Katharen!" Ms. Harner calls. "Katharen!"

but I don't stop.

RUIN, DISASTER

I run all the way to the office.
I don't stop for anyone.
They call Ms. Harner,
but it doesn't matter what she says.
I won't listen. I don't listen.
I say I'm not feeling well.
"No, I can't wait for the bell.
I want to go home.
I want to go home.
I want to go home now!"

Mama hurries. Mama comes.
"Keet? What's wrong?"

I can't tell her.
I get in the car
and I cry and cry.

"Baby, what's wrong?
What's wrong, Keet?
Tell me what's wrong."

I am Keet-Keet Parakeet
the story-talker, the story-maker.
I used to be. But not now.
They didn't like the stories.
They didn't like the teller.
They didn't want the heart-box
        inside of me.

HOME

I wake up,
curled in my bed.
Mama has tucked me in.

I hear voices
in the kitchen.

I hear Nose chitter-chattering
and asking someone to read to him.

I hear a deep breath.
Slowly, I open my eyes
and see Grandpa's walker.
And in my chair
I see—Grandpa!

I jump out of bed
to give him a hug.
"Are you better, Grandpa?"

"Well, I'm a little better now
that my Fisssh Bait's woken up.
I was w-worried about her."
His voice is raspy and not very loud.
He still says "Fish Bait" in a funny way.
But it's my grandpa's voice,
my Old Grandpa.

"I hear someone caught
a big fish today in school."

"No, Grandpa.
I didn't catch anything.
I tried to talk, but it came out wrong.
Everybody stared at me.
They think I talk funny."

"Fisssh Bait, I think I need
to take you night fishing."

"Night fishing? Can we really
go night fishing, Grandpa?
Are you getting better?"

"Better now that I see my Fisssh Bait smiling.
Makes me want to get up and start smiling too.
But right now, there's folks waiting
for you in the kitchen. They've been telling
me all about you, and they're waiting to see you."

"Who, Grandpa? Who wants to see me?"

AN UNEXPECTED VISITOR

Nose squeals, "Keet-y,"
and runs to me.

"You slept a long time, Keet-y.
I'm playing with Allie-gator.
She had supper with us.
Mama said you didn't want any supper.
She said you needed to sleep.
I gave Allie-gator your chocolate milk.
She drank it all up.
Look, Keet-y,
the Library Lady is here to see you.
She gave me a sticker.
See my sticker, Keet-y?"

At our table, across from Mama,
sits Ms. Lindle. My head
drops to my chin. I want
to run away again, but
I hear the stutter of Grandpa's walker.
He comes to the kitchen,
even though it makes his legs tremble,
even though it makes his arms shake.
Allie-gator gives me a wink,
but I don't know what it means.

"Am I in trouble?" I ask.

"Trouble? Oh, Katharen, no.
I heard your Dream Report today,
and I thought it was fabulous.
I wanted your family to know.
We were all so proud of you.
If you'd stayed, you would have
heard everyone clapping for you."

"They clapped?"

"Even John Royale," Allie-gator says.
"Yes, even John Royale." Ms. Lindle smiles.

"But I didn't give the right kind of report,"
I say. "It wasn't about what I wanted
to be when I grow up. It wasn't like
the other kids' reports."

"Well . . . maybe not. But Katharen,
you put marvelous pictures in our heads.
             We heard *you.*
There can't be anything braver than what you did,
or anything better. Well . . . maybe one thing.
Can you come to see me tomorrow,
since I came all this way to see you?"

I look at Grandpa,
I look at Mama,
and nod my head *yes.*

FISHING LESSON #8

I stick to Grandpa like glue,
like a stamp on a letter,
like a spider web,
like sticky tape.

I stick like a cocklebur.
I stick like a shadow.
I stick like a peanutbutterdillpickle sandwich.

I won't let him get away
ever again.

"Tell me about night fishing, Grandpa."

It takes Grandpa a while to start. His voice
is soft. And sometimes,
his words slip and slur.
Sometimes, he stops to catch his breath.
But then he looks at me, my Old Grandpa,
and starts again. He won't give up.

"If you want to catch the big fish, Fish Bait,
sometimes the best time to go is at night,
when the mosquitoes are singing,
when the air cools, and the moon
is a creamy bowl of buttermilk.

"Sometimes it's best to go fishing at night
when all the other fishers are at home snoring.
Go out and set your lines, your nets,
your traps. Then go away and come back
in the morning. Go night fishing, Fish Bait,

"because at night, the big fish come out, quietly
rising, quietly nib-nib-nibbling at your bait.
And when you go back early in the morning—
you'll find that you've caught some of the biggest
fish of all. Sometimes, fish don't come right away.
They don't come when you want them.
They like to take their time.
They swim slow and easy, slow and easy.
But if you're patient, if you come
at the right time, you'll find them."

"I ran away, Grandpa."

"You did. But the fish came anyway.
They liked your stories, Fish Bait.
You drew them in and caught them.
Just like you caught me."

THIS MIGHT INTEREST YOU

National contest . . .
Enter by . . .
Original . . .

"Katharen," Ms. Lindle says.
"I enjoyed your report.
You should write it down.
Here's something that might interest you."

National contest . . .
Enter by . . .
Original . . .

"See what you can do, Katharen.
I'm happy to help, if you have questions."

National contest . . .
Enter by . . .
Original . . .

A writing contest,
a short story contest.
After school, I go home,
and I write, and I write,
and I write.

National contest . . .
Enter by . . .
Original . . .

"Keet-Keet, time for supper."
"Katharen, time for bed."
"Keet, what are you working on so hard?
Keet? Keet-Keet? Katharen?
Put it away!"

National contest . . .
Enter by . . .
Original . . .

I write a lot and erase a lot.
I write and rewrite and try to get it right.
I write down all the words
that float, dizzy-dance,
and tumble in my head.

National contest . . .
Enter by . . .
Original . . .

The deadline is coming closer.

National contest . . .
Enter by . . .
Original . . .

Ms. Lindle helps me fill out the form.
Ms. Lindle sends my story in.

"It's a good story, Katharen."

"Really?" I ask.

"Absolutely-truly-ruly-
no-mistake-for-certain," Ms. Lindle says.

National contest . . .
Enter by . . .
Original . . .

WAITING

Waiting is the lace
on the collar of your dress that you have to wear to school,
and it scratches and itches, and scratches and itches:

    a long, long time.

Waiting is the nine bazillion hours before your favorite TV show,
the nine gazillion hours before school gets out,
and the nine padrillion days before your birthday:

    a long, long time.

Waiting is lying in bed at night when it's still dark,
and the house is all creaky,
and you can hear a moth flick-flick-flick against the window:

    a long, long time.

But Ms. Lindle says,
"We just have to wait, Katharen."

"How long?" I say.

Ms. Lindle looks at me.

I go back to reading
and doing my homework
and waiting,

waiting,

waiting.

NOAH'S BIG SURPRISE

Nose can't wait any longer.
"Keet-y, hurry up.
I want to show you something."

There on the kitchen table,
Mama, Grandpa,
Allie-gator, and I
see a large hump
covered with cloth.

Nose pulls the cloth away.
In her cage
sits Molly Cockatoo.

Nose pushes a peanut
through the bars.
"Say it, Molly," Nose says.

"Awk, Grandpa!
Awk, Grandpa!

"Hullo, Grandpa!
Awk! Hullo, Grandpa!"

"That's a mighty fine chicken,"
Grandpa says.

"No, Grandpa!" we all say.
"That's not a chicken!"

Mama laughs at me laughing,
at Noah laughing,
at Grandpa laughing,
at Molly squawking,

"Pretty girl!
Grandpa pretty girl!"

And Allie-gator smiles
her biggest s-m-i-l-e ever,
bright and pointy as a star.

Chapter 9

A TRILLION
WEEKS LATER

THE MYSTERY OF THE STRANGE SMILE

Everyone's acting strange.
Mama makes my favorite breakfast:
cornmeal pancakes with applesauce,
and hot chocolate with two extra
marshmallows, for no reason at all.

"Just because," she says.
And then she gives me a strange smile.

Grandpa talks and talks to Daddy
and hardly says a thing to me.

Even Daddy isn't acting right.
When he comes home from the road,
I always get to watch him shave.
He lets me pat-pat-pat the shaving cream
on his cheeks. But today, Daddy
just gives me a chicken-peck kiss,
a strange smile, and hurries off to work.

Even my teachers
act strange. After recess,
Ms. Harner marches us to the library.

"Why are we going to library?"
I ask Allegra. It's not library day.

"The principal has an announcement,"
Ms. Harner says,
and gives me a super-strange smile.

We're sitting in the reading circle
when the door opens,
and in walks the principal,
in walks
Mama,
Daddy,
Grandpa,
Nose,
Ms. Lindle,
and a man with a camera!

"Class, one of our students wrote a story
for a national contest," the principal says.
"Her story has won an honorable mention.
Our school is so proud of her.
Katharen, would you please come forward?"

Something silvery leaps inside me,
something cold and tickly.
I feel minnows and squiggly-wiggly tadpoles
swimming in my stomach.

The class cheers.

Grandpa waves his fishing hat.

Mama's eyes are watery pools.

Daddy puts a hand on my shoulder.

Noah makes the loudest noise of all.
"Keet-y! Keet-y! Keet-y!" he chants.

Allie-gator holds up a picture she's hidden
in her pocket: a girl with a heart shape
on her dress, and in the heart, a fish.

They put my picture in the paper.
They give me a certificate with a big red ribbon.
Ms. Lindle displays my story in the library
with a sign that says: *You're a Writer, Katharen Walker!*

HONORABLE MENTION

I ask Ms. Lindle
what "honorable mention" means.

She says I didn't win,
or get second place, or third,
but the judges think
I have talent.

"Winning isn't the important thing, Katharen.
The important thing is your stories.

"Keep telling them.
Write them down.
One day everyone will read them."

THE END OF THE STORY

"Keep writing, Keet-Keet, and who knows
what could happen," Mama says,
and she gives me a sloppy kiss
on the top of my head.

"Fish Bait, you caught your storyfish,"
Grandpa says. "Now hold on to it.
Hold on good and tight, and don't let go!"

"No, Grandpa, I won't let go."

Daddy doesn't say a thing,
but he brings me a notebook
where he's written my name,
and a silver pencil
with a fish-shaped eraser.
I give Daddy a hug
and go off to bed.
I think about the day
and all its surprises.

Keep telling stories.
It's not the winning. It's the writing.

I look at the midnight cup
on the shelf and think of the wishes
and secrets and memories it holds.
I look at the fish-shaped eraser.
I look inside my head and see Noah
with another cup of chocolate milk,
saying over and over, "Tell me a story, Keet-y."

And inside something
                    leaps, splashes light.
Something comes
                    and waits
for a line,
                    for a word,

            for a small whispering heart.

I lift my pencil,
open my notebook—and write.

POETRY GLOSSARY

Abecedarian

In an abecedarian poem, the first line begins with the letter
A, the second line with B, and so on through the alphabet.
Example: "Allegra Can Spell Anything."

Blues Poem

A blues poem uses or adapts the 12-bar rhyming structure of
the African-American music form called the blues. To write a
blues, write two similar or nearly similar lines that present a
problem. Then use the third line to respond to the problem.
The best way to write a blues poem is to listen to blues music.
Blues musicians and poets often play variations on the form,
as I do here.

> I got the New-Girl blues.
> I got those back-to-school and don't-want-to,
> do-I-have-to-Mama? do-I-have-to? blues.

Catalog Poem

A catalog poem is structured like a list. Often, a catalog poem
begins with a phrase that repeats again and again. This pattern
of repetition is called anaphora. Martin Luther King, Jr.'s
"I Have a Dream" speech offers a famous example of anaphora.
"Library Helper" is a catalog poem that uses anaphora. "Things
to Do with a Baby Brother" and "Sleepover" are also catalog
poems, but they do not use anaphora.

Concrete Poem

A concrete poem expresses its topic in the shaping of the words
on the page. For example, "Fishing Line Knot Hook" takes the
shape of a marshmallow on a fishhook.

Contrapuntal Poem

This is a difficult form. Readers can read a contrapuntal in three ways. The left column is one poem, and the right column is a second poem. When we read the whole poem from left to right, we find a third poem. Example: "Keet   Grandpa."

Haibun

This is a Japanese form composed of prose and a haiku. The haiku and the prose should enrich and expand each other. Example: "Cafeteria."

Haiku

This Japanese form gives the reader vivid images. Traditionally, American haiku have five syllables in the first line, seven in the second line, and five in the third line. Haiku usually say something about nature and seasonal change. The haiku in this book are closer to senryu, a variation of haiku that focuses more on people. Examples: "Do We Have To?," "Not Yet," "Allegra Wonders," and "Keet Wonders."

Narrative Poem

Narrative poems tell stories. Many of the poems in this book are narrative poems, including "Keet's Story for Noah" and "Keet's Story for Grandpa about the Terrible, Horrible, Kid-Eating Dog."

Pantoum

A pantoum repeats the second and fourth line of each quatrain as the first and third line of the following quatrain. (A quatrain is a four-line stanza.) Typically, pantoums have an *abab* rhyming pattern. "Keet's Wish" and "Allie-Gator's Wish" are pantoums but without the rhyme. Poets often experiment with words and poetic forms.

Prose poem

A prose poem is an experimental form that has no line breaks. A prose poem can have one or more paragraphs. Although a prose poem looks like prose, it still uses poetic language. Example: "Saturday: Fishing Lesson #6."

ACKNOWLEDGEMENTS

I especially want to thank my editor, Rebecca Davis, for her enthusiastic support and guidance. Thanks as well to all the people at WordSong, including Cherie Matthews and Lisa Rosinsky. *Catching a Storyfish* would not have been possible without my extraordinary agent, Stephen Fraser, and my readers: Betsy Hearne, Molly MacRae, and always Robert Dale Parker.